# Mean, Mean
# Maureen Green

# Mean, Mean Maureen Green

by Judy Cox

illustrated by Cynthia Fisher

Holiday House/New York

# To Mom and Dad

Text copyright ©1999 by Judy Cox
Illustrations copyright ©1999 by Cynthia Fisher
All Rights Reserved
Printed in the United States of America
FIRST EDITION

Library of Congress Cataloging-in-Publication Data
Cox, Judy.
Mean, mean Maureen Green / by Judy Cox;
illustrated by Cynthia Fisher. — 1st ed.
p.     cm.
Summary: With help from Adam, a boy in her third grade class,
Lilley gains enough confidence to stand up to the school bus bully,
Mean Maureen Green.
ISBN 0-8234-1502-3
[1. Bullies—Fiction. 2. Schools—Fiction. 3. School
buses—Fiction. 4. Fear—Fiction.]
I. Fisher, Cynthia, ill.   II. Title.
PZ7.C83535Me 2000
[Fic]—dc21                                99-11935
                                              CIP

# Contents

# 1. Watch Out for Maureen!

"Twenty-eight, twenty-nine, thirty!" Lilley chinned herself one last time and dropped to her feet. She rubbed her hands on her pants. She sniffed her palms. She liked the smell her hands got from the chin-up bar. Sort of metally.

It was the last day of summer vacation. But there were a lot of kids on the school playground. Like Lilley, they couldn't stay away.

Cassandra ran past, chasing a soccer ball. She skidded to a stop when she saw Lilley.

"Guess what!" she said. "This year Maureen's gonna ride your bus!"

Lilley felt pale. "What do you mean?"

1

Cassandra scooped up the ball. "They changed the bus route. Maureen's on your bus. Boy, am I glad she's not on mine! Know what she did last year?"

Lilley shook her head. She licked her lips.

"She gave a kid a swirly." Cassandra's eyes were wide.

"What's that?" asked Lilley. She leaned closer, not sure she wanted to hear.

"Maureen held a girl upside-down in the toilet and flushed!" Cassandra punched the soccer ball. "It made the girl's hair snarl."

Lilley shivered.

Ray ran over, followed by Suzanne. "Hey, Cass, we're waiting for the ball!" he said.

"Maureen's gonna be on Lilley's bus this year."

Ray's eyes got big. "Maureen Green? Isn't she a fifth-grader?"

"Fourth," said Cassandra.

"What's that?" asked Suzanne. "Maureen's on Bus Thirty this year? Mean, mean Maureen Green?"

All the kids talked at once. "I heard she stuffed a kid in a garbage can," said one.

"Oh, yeah! The kid was covered with slime for the rest of the day!"

## Watch Out for Maureen!

"Yuck!"

Ray nodded. "Yeah, and if she asks for your lunch—man! You better give it to her. Fast. Or else!"

Cassandra shook her head. "I feel sorry for you, Lilley Nelson."

She drop-kicked the soccer ball. The kids pelted after it, leaving Lilley alone.

Cassandra called over her shoulder, "Watch out for Maureen!"

Lilley's mouth turned down. The good feeling of doing thirty chin-ups melted like a snowflake in the sun.

# 2. The Bully on the Bus

The next day, Dad dropped Lilley off at school. So she didn't ride the bus until school was out.

The first day of third grade went by quickly. Mrs. Johnson turned out to be Lilley's favorite kind of teacher, friendly and full of smiles. Cassandra was in her class. And a new boy with glasses.

In fact, school was so interesting, Lilley almost forgot about Maureen. But not quite.

At lunch, Lilley sat next to Cassandra. Lilley took a bite out of her sandwich. Yum. Peanut butter.

Cassandra watched. "I don't know how you can eat," she said. "Aren't you scared? In just a few short hours—the bus! Maureen!"

Lilley put her sandwich down. Suddenly, she wasn't hungry.

At last, it was time to go home.

Lilley's knees trembled as she climbed the bus stairs. Front seats were safest, close to the driver. But when Lilley got on board, all the front seats were full. Nathan and Joel shared a seat. So did Alex and Amy. It seemed everyone else had heard Maureen would ride Bus Thirty, too.

Lilley walked to the back of the bus, the very back. Her feet dragged as slowly as a prisoner on her way to execution. Only the very last seat was empty. She slid in.

Lilley heard Maureen before she saw her. STOMP, STOMP, STOMP. When Maureen walked, the whole bus shook.

Maureen sailed down the aisle like the *Titanic*. Her fists were the size of catcher's mitts. Her shoulders looked like a quarterback's. Her nose was as kinked as a prizefighter's.

Lilley curled up against the window. If only she could turn into a mouse. If only Maureen wouldn't see her.

But Maureen stopped in the aisle right in front of Lilley.

"Hey, kid!" she growled. Lilley peered up. "Out. This is my seat."

Lilley uncurled herself and slipped out of the seat. She slid past Maureen and squeezed into the seat with Hannah and Jenny.

Maureen plunked down.

"Listen up!" she yelled. The noisy bus was suddenly silent.

Her voice echoed. "From now on, the backseat is my seat! I own this seat!"

No one disagreed.

"Can it, Maureen," muttered the bus driver. "Nine different routes and I have to get this one."

With a clash of gears and a belching roar, the bus lurched off. Little by little, talking started up again. Lilley sighed. Safe for now.

Lilley got off the bus and dashed down the sidewalk. She pounded up the stairs and flung open the door. Home. Now she didn't have to think about Maureen for the rest of the day.

Mrs. Blick, the housekeeper, was in the kitchen. She wore a purple jogging suit and earrings to match.

Lilley slid onto the stool at the counter. She tore open a bag of potato chips. Mrs. Blick took the chips away. She gave Lilley an apple and a glass of milk. Lilley sighed.

"I bought you something," said Mrs. Blick.

She pushed over a brown paper sack. "I hope you don't have this already."

"Oh, goody!" Lilley ripped open the sack and pulled out a box of cornflakes. On the front of the box was a big orange tiger wearing a bandanna.

"A tiger!" cried Lilley. "I can't wait to add it to my collection! Thanks!" She ran around the counter to hug Mrs. Blick. Her arms barely reached around her waist.

"You're welcome, dear." Mrs. Blick patted Lilley's head. "When I saw the tiger on the box, I couldn't resist. Heaven knows you don't need more tigers. You must have a hundred by now. Go on with you, now. Finish your apple."

Lilley returned to the stool. She bit into her apple.

"How was school?" Mrs. Blick stacked cans of beans in the cupboard.

While Mrs. Blick's back was turned, Lilley
sneaked a handful of chips. "Okay. They changed the
bus route."

A lumped formed in Lilley's throat. The chips
wouldn't go down. "Maureen rides my bus."

"Maureen?"

"You know! Mean, mean Maureen Green." Lilley's
voice sank to a whisper. "They say she put a tarantula

on a kid's head and it bit him. I think it killed him or something."

Mrs. Blick stopped putting away groceries. She shook her head, and her purple earrings danced. "Well, I wouldn't worry about Maureen."

But Lilley didn't hear. She pictured a tarantula crawling down her hair and inside the collar of her shirt. Did you die all at once or would it take a long time?

Suddenly Lilley wasn't hungry. She put down her half-eaten apple. She slid off the stool.

"I've got homework!" she called. She dashed upstairs to her bedroom, taking the cereal box with her.

Upstairs, Lilley went to her bookshelf where she kept her collection. Tigers of every shape and size crouched on the shelves. Lilley carefully set the corn-flake box behind a tiger pencil box. She swiped the dust off a plastic tiger.

Now she had forty-seven tigers, each one different. There were stuffed tigers with friendly faces. China figurines with painted whiskers. Paper tigers and tiger books and even a wind-up toy tiger. Lilley had tiger mugs, a tiger backpack, and tiger T-shirts.

She couldn't remember why or even when she had started collecting tigers. But she knew which tiger was her favorite.

It was Stripe. He was so old his fur was nearly worn off. His whiskers had fallen out long ago. Mrs. Blick had sewn on pipe-cleaner whiskers to replace them. Lilley picked him up. She sprawled on her bed and gave him a squeeze.

Holding Stripe calmed her. She rolled off the bed to change for dinner. She hoped Mrs. Blick wouldn't tell Dad about Maureen. She knew what he would say.

"I hear you're worried about the new bus route," said Dad. He took a bite of green beans.

"It isn't so much the route," Lilley admitted. "It's Maureen."

Dad looked up from his plate. His eyebrows came up. His eyebrows always did that when Lilley was supposed to say something. It was like saying, "Well?" with his face.

Lilley pushed the green beans around her plate. "She's bigger than I am."

Dad's eyebrows were still up. He waited for Lilley to say more.

Lilley made a face at her beans. "Well, she is. Everybody knows she's supposed to be in fifth grade this year, but she got held back. I'm only a third-grader. And she's mean, Dad. They say she likes to fight. I don't want to fight."

Dad took a sip of water. "I don't expect you to fight!" He laughed. "Maybe she just wants to be

friends and doesn't know how. Why don't you try making friends with her?"

Lilley's eyes widened. "Dad! Maureen doesn't make friends. She takes prisoners!"

Dad laughed. "I'm sure she isn't all that bad. She's only ten, after all."

"Oh, Dad, you don't know Maureen. She beats up people, even big kids. Once, she hit a girl and knocked out two teeth! Permanent teeth!"

Dad shook his head. "Sounds like you've been listening to gossip," he said. He took a sip of water and looked straight at Lilley.

"Besides," he said, "you don't have to ride the bus to school. You could ride your new bike."

Lilley tried to swallow, but the green beans stuck in her throat. The bike. No matter what the problem was, Dad always came back to the bike.

# 3. The Purple Bike

After dinner, Lilley sat on the floor of her bedroom, in her flannel pj's with pink bunnies on them. She sorted her tigers. All the stuffed animals in one pile. All the rest in another.

But the tigers didn't help. Her thoughts still buzzed like bees around honey.

Dad always came back to the bike.

He had given her the bike two weeks ago, on her eighth birthday.

"One last surprise," he said, after she'd opened all her presents. He put his hands over her eyes and led her to the garage.

"Surprise!" he yelled, pulling his hands away.

## The Purple Bike

A new bike. And what a bike!

Purple paint! Silver wheels! A kickstand. A horn that went *Ooh-ga! Ooh-ga!* A chain and lock. Two wheels.

Two wheels. No training wheels.

"Gee, Dad, thanks," said Lilley in a quiet voice. "A bike. Swell."

"It will be great, Lilley! We can go on rides together! And look at this!" He plopped a new helmet on Lilley's head.

"But, Dad," said Lilley. "It doesn't have training wheels."

Dad laughed. "Of course not, Lilley. Training wheels? You're too big for training wheels. I'll teach you to ride today, and Saturday we'll ride the river road. It's only five miles and the hills aren't too steep."

Lilley swallowed. Five miles. Hills. No training wheels. "Maybe I could ride my old bike."

"You're much too big for your old bike. I gave it to Goodwill. Come on, what do you say we have our first lesson right now?" Dad smiled down at her.

"I haven't finished my cake yet."

That was two weeks ago. She still hadn't asked Dad to teach her to ride the new bike.

The next morning, Lilley ran all the way to the bus stop. She wanted to be the first on the bus. She wanted to sit as far from Maureen as possible. But when she got to the bus stop, someone else was already there.

It was the new kid. Black hair curled over his ears. Glasses slid down his nose. He wore a sweatshirt with a hood.

He reached into his pocket and scooped out a handful of something and dropped it on the ground. Then he did it again. Lilley stared.

Each time the boy dipped his hand into his pocket, he pulled something out and threw it on the ground. Lilley couldn't see what it was.

"Why are you doing that?" she asked.

"Because I don't like oatmeal," he replied.

He caught Lilley's eye and laughed. "See?"

Lilley moved closer. Thick gray goo oozed between his fingers.

"Every morning Mom gives me oatmeal for breakfast. But I fool her! I stick it in my pockets!" He shook his fingers. Blobs of oatmeal spattered the sidewalk.

Lilley nodded. She didn't like oatmeal, either.

"Doesn't your mom notice when she does the laundry?"

The boy pushed his glasses back on his nose

with his wrist. "She never checks my pockets," he said. "She says she's afraid of what she might find." He wiped his hands on his jeans. They left thick, white streaks on his pants.

"I'm Adam. Say, aren't you in Mrs. Johnson's class, too?"

"Yes," said Lilley. Just then, the bus pulled up with a groan. The doors crashed open.

Through the window Lilley could see Maureen in the backseat.

"Come on," said Adam.

"Don't sit in the back," whispered Lilley.

Adam slid into a seat halfway down the aisle. Lilley slid in next to him.

"Why not the back?" asked Adam.

"Maureen," she whispered. "Mean, mean Maureen Green. You know what she does?"

Adam shook his head.

"Once she made a kid eat mud! Right on the playground!" Lilley shuddered.

Adam laughed. Lilley looked at him in wonder. He didn't seem a bit scared.

"We had a bully like that in Boston," he said.

"They aren't so tough. My dad says you just have to stand up to them, that's all."

Lilley sneaked a peek at the backseat. Maureen saw her. She raised her right hand, and very slowly curled each finger into a fist. She shook it right at Lilley. Lilley shivered.

"I don't think I want to stand up to Maureen," she said in a little voice.

At lunchtime, Lilley sat between Cassandra and Adam. She unzipped her lunchbox. What had Mrs. Blick packed today? Yum! Rice cakes with peanut butter!

"What do you have?" she asked.

"Boring bologna," said Cassandra. "As usual." She sighed.

"Chopped-olive sandwiches and a lemon cupcake," said Adam.

"Chopped-olive sandwiches?" asked Cassandra. "That's weird."

"Yeah, my mom makes it. It was her favorite when she was a kid." He opened the bread to show the olives inside. They were black and shiny.

"Ugh," said Lilley. "It looks like beetles. Chopped beetles."

Adam giggled. "Yeah, right!" He made his voice go all high and squeaky. "I have a delicious chopped-beetle sandwich," he said. "Care to have a bite?"

Lilley shook her head. "No way."

"What do you have, Lilley?"

Rice cakes and peanut butter didn't sound exciting.

"Creamed earthworms," she said. She giggled. "On a crisp bed of deep-fried grasshoppers."

Adam laughed so hard, he snorted. Milk dribbled down his chin. That made them laugh harder. Even Cassandra laughed. They laughed so hard, the duty teacher shushed them.

Lilley looked up. Maureen stood in the doorway. She narrowed her eyes and stared around the room.

"Ooh," whispered Adam. He giggled. "Mean Maureen. Do you think she likes chopped beetles?"

To Lilley's horror, he stood up, holding out his sandwich. "Hey, Maureen! Chopped beetles! Want a bite?"

Lilley's heart pounded.

"Are you crazy?" she whispered.

She pulled him back down.

Maureen stared right at them. Any minute now, Maureen would march over and grab Lilley's lunch and Lilley would be helpless to do anything about it.

But the duty teacher saw Maureen first.

"Maureen Green! Get down to the office this instant! You're in detention all week, remember?"

Maureen growled and turned around.

Lilley's heart slowed. What a relief! She bit into her rice cake and chewed.

Adam tugged her sleeve. "I don't think she wanted my sandwich," he grinned. "She must be allergic to bugs."

He giggled, but Lilley didn't. It was too close a call.

# 4. The Great Cookie Caper

Saturday morning, Lilley pounded downstairs in her pink pj's. She poured herself a big bowl of Frosted Yummies.

Mrs. Blick wore a green jogging suit today. Her earrings were green to match.

She made gagging noises when she saw Lilley's breakfast. "Why don't you let me make you some nice oatmeal?"

Lilley laughed, remembering Adam dumping oatmeal out of his pockets.

Dad filled his water bottles at the sink. He wore bike shorts and narrow shoes. "Today's the sixty-mile loop with the Wheelmen," he said.

The Wheelmen was Dad's bike club. Every week-end he rode with them.

He smiled at Lilley. "I can't wait until you can ride, too. Say, how about a lesson this afternoon?"

Lilley paused, her spoon halfway to her mouth. She didn't want a bike-riding lesson. "Can't, Dad," she said. "I'm going to Adam's house."

Dad's face fell. "Whenever you're ready, Tiger." He kissed the top of Lilley's head and left.

Lilley felt bad. Dad called her Tiger, but she felt more like a mouse.

The last time she rode a bike was when she was four years old. She pedaled really fast. She hit the curb and lost control. She tried to put her foot down, but it got trapped in the spokes of the wheel.

Dad took her to the hospital for an X ray. Her broken arm was in a cast for six weeks. Lilley hadn't been on a bike since.

Now, she left her bowl on the table and ran upstairs to get dressed.

"What are you going to do at Adam's house?" Mrs. Blick called.

"LEGOs!" Lilley yelled back. "He's got a new set!"

Adam waited on the front steps. A little girl dressed in a red cape twirled on the sidewalk in front of him.

"Who's she?" the girl demanded when she saw Lilley.

"I'm Lilley. What's your name?"

"Sally Ann Levy. But you can call me Super Sal. And this is my invisible cape." Sally held out her cape. A big yellow S decorated the back.

"It's not invisible," said Adam. "I can see it."

"No, silly," said Sally. "The cape isn't invisible. I'm invisible."

"I can see you, too," said Adam. "But I don't want to. Why don't you go watch TV?" He pushed his glasses up.

"Don't want to," said Sally. "What are you guys doing?"

"LEGOs," said Lilley. "Want to play?"

"No!" said Adam. "She can't play with us. Go away."

Sally swirled the cape around her and stalked off. "I'm telling Mom!" she shouted.

Adam sighed. He pushed his glasses back. "Little sisters are a pain," he said. "You are so lucky to be an only child."

Lilley looked at the ground. Sometimes it didn't feel so lucky. Mostly there was just her and Dad and Mrs. Blick. Mom lived in California, and Lilley only saw her on vacations.

"Let's go to my treehouse," said Adam. He ran to the backyard.

There was only one tree in the backyard. It was tall, with big branches. A few leaves had turned yellow. Lilley saw boards nailed to a limb above their heads.

"Wow!" said Lilley. "How do we get up?"

Adam pointed to three wood blocks nailed into the trunk. Then he swarmed up the tree like a monkey. He disappeared from view, then leaned over the side.

"Come on!" he said.

Lilley set the LEGO bucket on the ground. "What about these?"

"Just a minute." Adam disappeared again. A rope snaked down from the branches and dangled in front of Lilley.

"Tie the rope to the handle!" he called.

"Okay!" Lilley pulled the rope through the handle and tied it in a bow. She gave two tugs. "Haul 'er up!"

Adam pulled the LEGO bucket up. There was a tense moment when Lilley's bow came loose, but Adam grabbed the bucket before it fell. "I've got to teach you to tie better knots," he said, laughing.

Lilley laughed, too. She climbed up the trunk.

"Wow," she said, when she reached the top.

Once, Lilley and Dad had hiked through a park. The trail went right behind a waterfall. The water rushed down in front of them like a lacy curtain. This treehouse was like that. A waterfall of leaves.

Lilley scoped out Adam's backyard. A sandbox, a tricycle, a black bike on its side. She looked over the fence to the yard next door. It looked like a long way down.

"Cool, huh?" said Adam.

"Did you build this?" asked Lilley.

Adam shook his head. "It was here when we moved in." Adam squatted and reached into the bucket of LEGOs.

He snapped two LEGOs together.

"I'm making a caterpillar!" he said. "For Maureen."

He made his voice go squeaky. "Hey, Maureen? Want a caterpillar sandwich?" He laughed.

Lilley was shocked. Maureen was nothing to joke about.

"Come on, Lilley," said Adam. "You make one."

Reluctantly, Lilley snapped some LEGOs together.

"Hey, Maureen!" Adam yelled. "Have some crocodile claws?"

Lilley couldn't help herself. She giggled.

Adam scooped up a handful of LEGOs.

"Cockroach eggs? Chocolate-covered ants? Fried grasshoppers?" His shoulders shook with giggles.

"Spider cookies?" said Lilley. She giggled so hard, her eyes scrunched up.

"Wait a minute!" Adam stood up. LEGOs streamed between his fingers. "I have a great idea!"

"What! What?"

Adam pushed his glasses on his nose. His blue eyes sparkled. "It's a trick. To play on Maureen."

He slid down the tree trunk. "Wait here."

Soon he was back. He held up a bag. "Look!"

Inside were three chocolate cream-filled cookies and a tube of toothpaste.

Lilley shook her head. "What are you doing?"

Adam laughed. He unscrewed the top half of one cookie and scraped the white frosting out with his finger. He licked it off and squirted white toothpaste onto the cookie. Then he put the top of the cookie back on. It looked almost the same as it had. But it didn't smell the same.

"Maureen?" He squeaked. "Want a cookie?"

Lilley's eyes widened. "Oh!" she yelled. "Let me make one!"

Lilley made one, and then Adam made another. They put the cookies in the brown paper bag.

"Let's take them to Maureen's house," said Adam. "And try them out."

Lilley gasped. "Are you crazy? She'd kill us! And anyway, I don't know where she lives."

"Okay, then. Monday," said Adam. "We'll try it Monday. On the bus."

Lilley shook her head again. "No way, Adam," she said. "You must have a death wish. You know what she does to kids who play tricks on her!"

Adam pushed his glasses up on his nose. "Lilley, you are such a wimp. Maureen's not so tough. Those kind of bullies only bug kids who are scared of them."

But Lilley wasn't sure. Maureen was bad news. Everybody said so.

Everybody but Adam.

# 5. Bruno

Late Monday afternoon, the bus was nearly empty. Most of the kids had already been dropped off. Maureen sat in the back. Adam and Lilley sat together, halfway back.

Adam held up the brown paper bag. He giggled.

Lilley shook her head.

"Yes," said Adam. "I'm going to do it."

"You are crazy!" Lilley grabbed for the bag.

Adam snatched it out of reach. He moved, seat by seat, to the back. Lilley watched in horror.

"Maureen? Want a cookie?" Adam held out the rumpled paper bag. He looked back at Lilley. His lips were pressed tightly together so no giggles could escape, but his eyes shone.

Maureen frowned at the bag. Then she shrugged.

"Okay, punk. But this doesn't mean we're friends." She reached in and pulled out a cookie.

Lilley watched Maureen bring the cookie up to her mouth. Her hand seemed to move in slow motion. Lilley hated watching, but she couldn't look away.

Maureen's teeth crunched through the chocolate layers. Down into the toothpaste. Toothpaste squirted out. She licked her lips.

Her smile changed. Her lips curled up. She pulled the cookie away and stared at it. "Yuck!"

Adam doubled over with laughter. He grabbed the sack and shoved it at Maureen.

"Like it?" He choked out the words. "Want another?"

Maureen spit out bits of cookie and toothpaste. Crumbs of chocolate flew everywhere. Her lips were covered with white foam. She looked like a mad dog. She doubled her fists and grabbed the sack from Adam.

"You little pip-squeak! You turkey! What is it?"

"Toothpaste!" shouted Adam. The bus lurched to a stop. The doors opened. Adam ran down the aisle, leaping the steps. Once outside, he turned around.

"Toothpaste cookies! Famous Lilley and Adam Toothpaste Cookies!" He danced off down the street.

Lilley's heart squeezed with terror. Lilley and Adam cookies! Oh no! Adam told Maureen she'd helped with the cookies, and then he ran off! She had to get away before Maureen could grab her.

But Maureen filled the aisle. Lilley couldn't get past.

"Let's go," said the bus driver in a tired voice. "Your stop, Lilley."

Maureen's face flushed. She stood in the aisle, flexing her fists.

This was awful. Lilley looked at the bus driver. The bus driver didn't see. Her eyes were closed.

A car pulled up behind the bus. "Maureen Green!"

Maureen looked out the bus window.

"Get in this car right now! You're late for swim-team practice!" yelled the driver.

Maureen ran down the bus stairs and slid into the passenger seat.

She was gone. The coast was clear. Lilley got off the bus.

But the car was still there. Maureen rolled down the window.

"You're dead meat, Lilley Nelson!"

Lilley ran all the way home.

The vacuum roared when Lilley got home. Mrs. Blick's jogging suit was orange today. She wore big orange earrings shaped like pumpkins. They jangled as she vacuumed.

Mrs. Blick had her headphones on, so Lilley just waved.

She grabbed a banana and ran upstairs. Dad wouldn't be home until dinner. She needed a plan before then.

She threw her backpack on her bed and pulled Stripe off the shelf. She needed to think.

She couldn't ride the bus to school tomorrow.

*Dead meat*, Maureen had said.

Lilley pictured Maureen's fist driving straight at her nose. She shuddered.

She could stay home and pretend to be sick. But Dad might take her to the doctor. Besides, she didn't want to lie.

She could ask Mrs. Blick to drive her to school. But Mrs. Blick would grumble and tell Dad, and Dad would point out she wouldn't have to ride the bus if she rode her bike.

If she could ride her bike.

But she couldn't ride her bike!

She finished the banana and poked the skin into

her rat cage. Harry, her rat, came out of his shoe-box house. He sniffed the skin.

Lilley pressed her nose against the glass of Harry's cage. She watched him drag the banana peel into his shoe box. Lucky rat. Rats didn't have to ride the bus. Rats didn't have to ride bikes. They just walked.

Wait a minute! Maybe she could walk to school!

Walking was safer than bike riding. It was good exercise. It was fresh air.

She was in third grade, after all. Since Dad thought she was old enough to ride her bike to school, he surely would let her walk.

But just to be safe, she wouldn't tell him.

The next morning, Dad left for work early. He kissed the top of her head as she finished her Yummies.

"See you tonight, Tiger," he said. He wore a red tie. His shoes were shiny and he smelled good. Lilley smiled.

Mrs. Blick arrived just as Dad left.

"Have a good day, Mr. Nelson," she said. Her earrings were purple again. So were her sweats and the stripes on her sneakers.

"What do you want for lunch today?" she asked.

"Creamed earthworms on deep-fried grasshoppers," said Lilley, giggling.

She felt good. No more Maureen. Her chest felt light. She floated like a balloon.

"Smarty," said Mrs. Blick.

Mrs. Blick was never at her best in the mornings. She made Lilley's lunch and packed it in Lilley's red plaid lunchbox.

Lilley grabbed her sweater. She shoved the lunchbox in her backpack and ran out the door. But she didn't go to the bus stop.

She didn't want anyone on the bus to see her, so she hid in the bushes.

Lilley watched the bus pull up. No Adam. Maybe he's sick, thought Lilley.

When the bus rumbled away, Lilley started off, swinging her sweater and whistling. She felt good. She felt alive. Why hadn't she done this before?

Two blocks from home, she passed a big old house with pointy towers. It would make a perfect haunted house. She slowed down to look.

Suddenly, a big black dog bounded around the

corner of the house. He stopped behind the fence and growled.

Lilley stopped. The dog glared at her between broken fence boards. His teeth were huge and sharp.

He snarled. Lilley stepped back. Should she run? Dad said never run away. The dog would chase you and you might get bit. But this dog was locked up. Wasn't he?

The dog raced to the far end of the yard, out of Lilley's sight, behind the fence.

Lilley let out a breath. He was gone.

She took a step forward.

The dog burst through a hole in the fence. And lunged straight at her!

# 6. The Big Black Bike

Lilley's feet were like blocks of ice. She wanted to run, but she couldn't move.

The dog stood directly in her path. Hair bristled on his neck. He snarled. Lilley could see his pointed teeth. She knew nothing about dogs. Was he a Doberman? Maybe he was a pit bull!

What could she do? She couldn't get by him.

And every minute made her late for school.

Could she throw her lunchbox at him? Maybe he would eat her lunch and not bite her. But when she raised her arm, he growled.

"Nice doggy," she tried. Her voice trembled.

"Bruno!"

Lilley heard footsteps on the porch, but she couldn't look. She was afraid to take her eyes off the dog.

"Hold still, little girl," she heard a man say. "Don't move."

Easy to obey. Lilley couldn't move.

"Steady now, Bruno." The man grabbed Bruno by his collar.

Bruno's claws skidded on the sidewalk as the man dragged him through the gate.

"How did you get loose?" The man snapped a chain onto Bruno's collar.

Bruno curled his lips. His sharp teeth glistened. "Wait—just wait—until next time," he seemed to say.

Lilley's happy, balloon feeling disappeared. She walked past the house and broke into a run.

She ran the rest of the way to school. Four blocks. No one was on the playground. Even the halls were empty. She had to go to the office for a late pass.

She hated getting a late pass. Everyone stared.

Adam sat next to Lilley at lunch.

## The Big Black Bike

The cafeteria was so noisy he nearly had to shout. "Where were you?" he asked. "Why were you late?"

She told him about the dog.

"I didn't see you at the bus stop," she said.

Adam grinned. "Are you kidding? Ride the bus, with Maureen on the warpath? No way! I rode my bike. Walking's too slow."

The bike again. Lilley stared at her carrot sticks. Her shoulders slumped.

"Why don't you ride, too?" asked Adam. "You have a bike, don't you?"

"Course I do." Lilley didn't want to tell him she couldn't ride. Probably everybody in third grade could ride. Everybody but her.

"Let's ride to school tomorrow. I know a shortcut. No dogs," Adam said.

Lilley poked her carrot sticks. "I can't ride," she muttered.

"Huh?" said Adam.

Lilley glared at him. "I can't ride. I don't know how!"

Adam pushed his glasses up on his nose. "Why doncha learn then? I'll teach you! After school. On the playground."

Lilley rolled a carrot stick between her fingers.

"Come on," said Adam. "Why not?"

Bloody knees, thought Lilley. Bloody elbows. Scraped shins. Sprained ankles. Broken arms.

"I don't know, Adam. Maybe not."

Adam gave her a disgusted look. "Don't be a wimp, Lilley. Meet me on the playground after the bus leaves. You don't want to ride the bus, do you? With Maureen?"

• • •

It seemed like school would never end. Then quite suddenly, the bell rang. Mrs. Johnson's class lined up for the bus.

Cassandra ran past the door. "I'm getting picked up!" she shouted. "Dentist appointment!"

Lilley dragged her backpack out to the playground. In the field, Suzanne and Ray kicked the soccer ball around. Andy hung upside-down on the monkey bars. The buses left.

Soon the playground was deserted. Lilley waited. What was taking so long?

She hoped the bike wouldn't be too big.

Adam wheeled his bike out. It was big. Big and black.

"Come on," he said impatiently. "Are you going to ride or not?"

"I don't know yet," said Lilley. "Don't rush me."

Adam sighed noisily, blowing air out of his nose like a horse.

Lilley stalled. She grabbed the chin-up bar.

"Twenty-eight, twenty-nine," she chanted. "Thirty!"

She dropped to the ground and rubbed her hands together. She sniffed her palms.

Adam whistled. "Wow! I bet even Maureen can't do thirty chin-ups!"

Lilley grinned. "I like chin-ups," she said shyly. "But it's the only thing I'm good at."

Adam pointed to the bike. "Well, if you can do thirty chin-ups, you can ride a two-wheeler. Come on, Lilley."

Lilley took a deep breath. She tried to picture herself spinning down the road like Dad.

"Here." Adam plopped something hard on her head.

She pulled the helmet into place. Adam showed her how to fasten the straps.

"Get on," Adam said. "I'll hold the bike."

Lilley climbed on the bike. Her feet barely touched the ground.

"Put your feet on the pedals," said Adam.

Adam held the bike. Lilley lifted her feet and put them on the pedals.

"You're heavier than Sally," Adam said. He tried to hold the bike steady. "Now, push down with one foot."

"Don't let go," she said. "Promise."

"I won't," said Adam.

Lilley lifted up her foot and pushed down. Adam tried to hold the bike and push at the same time. But it was too heavy. It wobbled.

The bike crashed over. Lilley tumbled off. Her ankle twisted under her leg.

"You let go!" she wailed.

She grabbed her ankle and held it, rocking back and forth.

Adam looked pained.

"Well, you weigh a ton! Anyway, kids aren't supposed to teach kids to ride. Why don't you ask your dad? My dad taught me."

He sounded mad. He picked up his bike and checked it for scratches.

Lilley sniffed. Blood trickled down her knee. Probably her ankle was broken. All Adam cared about was his bike.

"Are you okay?" Adam asked gruffly.

Lilley moved her ankle. It didn't hurt anymore. Not much. She nodded.

"But I don't want to ride anymore." Lilley unstrapped Adam's helmet.

Adam took his helmet back.

"You're a wimp, Lilley," he said, grumpily. "Face it."

## The Big Black Bike

Lilley folded her arms across her chest. She stuck out her chin.

Adam climbed on his bike. He pedaled away. He crouched low over the handlebars and jumped the curb.

"So much for you, Adam Levy!" Lilley yelled. "I thought you were my friend!"

# 7. Tiger Lilley

The buses were gone. Lilley called Mrs. Blick from the school office and asked her to pick her up.

Mrs. Blick was mad. "Lilley!" she scolded when she pulled up in front of the school. "What's this all about? I was just about to put the roast in the oven when you called. Now there won't be time to cook it. And you know how your father feels about under-done meat!"

Lilley only half listened. She was more worried about what Dad would say.

• • •

When they got home, Lilley ran upstairs. She threw herself on the bed. "This is the worst day of my life," she moaned.

What should she do? If she rode the bus, Maureen would beat her up. If she walked, Bruno would eat her up.

Tap, tap. Dad peeked around the door. "May I come in?" he asked. He held a package.

Lilley nodded.

Dad sat on the bed. He picked up Stripe. "I remember this guy," he said. "Mom and I bought Stripe for your third birthday. It was the beginning of your tiger collection."

Lilley raised herself up and sat next to him. He handed her the package.

"I brought you a present," he said. "And I have a story to tell you."

Lilley unwrapped the package. A pair of fuzzy orange socks with black stripes fell out.

"Tiger socks," said Dad. "For my tiger."

Lilley didn't feel like a tiger. More like a mouse.

"When you were three, you were the fiercest little girl I ever saw," said Dad. "You weren't afraid of

anything. I was always terrified you'd get hurt. You
tore around the house like a wild beast, climbing on
tables, jumping off swings."

"Is that how I got my nickname?" asked Lilley.

"Yes," said Dad. "Mom and I called you Tiger because you were so wild." He laughed. "I don't know how you lived to be eight."

Lilley burrowed under his arm.

"I'm not fierce now," she said.

He squeezed her shoulders.

"People change as they grow up," he said. "You learned to be more cautious. That's good. We don't want to haul you to the hospital every day."

He patted the tiger socks. "But you must find some of that courage you used to have. When you put on these socks, think to yourself: Brave Lilley. Tiger Lilley."

He nodded. "Then you can face up to some of your fears."

Lilley pulled the striped socks on. Could socks give you courage? She sighed. She was too old to believe that. But how could she find the courage she'd lost?

She wiggled her toes. Her feet felt warm and cozy.

At once, the feeling of doing chin-ups flooded back. Hanging halfway between earth and sky, holding on with just your hands. And the muscles in your arms bulge and your palms hurt, but you don't let go, because you can do it.

"You can do it, Lilley," she whispered. "You can do it. Mouse no more. Tiger Lilley."

She took a deep breath.

"Dad," she said, "teach me to ride my bike."

Dad's eyebrows went up. He smiled.

"Of course!" he said. "Right after dinner." He beamed at Lilley. "Tiger! This will be great!"

Lilley looked at her socks. Her feet still felt warm. But suddenly, she didn't have much appetite.

# 8. Don't Let Go

Dad held the bike steady while Lilley climbed on. She took a deep breath.

"Don't let go," she told him. "Promise."

But Dad laughed. "No, Lilley, we aren't riding yet. I just want to measure your legs and adjust the seat."

He checked to make sure she could put her feet down. Then she got off while he did something to the bicycle seat with a wrench. He hummed as he worked.

Lilley was glad he was happy. But her chest was tight. Her hands were cold.

Dad looked up. His eyes twinkled.

"There," he said. "I think that's it."

Lilley took a deep breath. Time to ride. She tried not to think about broken arms. Twisted ankles. Blood.

But Dad wasn't ready yet.

"My, you're in a hurry." He laughed. "Don't forget your helmet."

He handed Lilley the new helmet. Lilley put it on. Dad showed her how to pinch the clips together to fasten the straps. Then he made her take it off so he could adjust it.

Waiting made Lilley nervous. "Come on, Dad," she wanted to say. "Just do it!"

But Dad could not be hurried. He hummed a little tune. He adjusted Lilley's helmet. Finally, he pushed her bike down the driveway and into the street.

"Always ride with traffic," he told her. "On the right side of the street. That way cars can see you."

Lilley climbed onto her bike. Her toes trailed on the ground.

"Remember your coaster brakes," he told her. "All you have to do is push the pedals backward and the bike will stop. You're in control."

No, I'm not, thought Lilley.

"What if somebody sees me?" she whispered. "Everybody else already knows how to ride a bike."

Dad looked up and down the street. "There's nobody out here but us," he said.

Lilley took another deep breath. She gripped the handlebars until her knuckles turned white.

"Okay," she said, in a tight voice.

Dad held the bike steady. He put one hand on the handlebars. One hand on the seat. The bike didn't wobble like it had when Adam tried to hold it.

"Put your feet on the pedals," he told her. "And push down."

Lilley pushed with her left foot. The bike sped forward. Dad raced along beside, holding the back of the seat. Lilley pedaled. Up and down. Up and down.

The street looked only inches from her toes. Look up, she told herself.

"Don't let go," she yelled. "Promise!"

But Dad didn't answer. Dad wasn't holding on anymore. He ran along the sidewalk, grinning and waving.

"You're riding, Lilley!" he yelled. "You're riding!"

Energy surged through Lilley like an electric shock.

I'm riding! By myself! Really! It felt like flying. She skimmed along the street. Her feet flashed up and down on the pedals. Up and down.

Then she fell off.

One minute, she swooped along the street. The next minute, she sprawled on the ground. The bike sprawled next to her. The wheels spun. Her hands burned, but she grinned as Dad ran up.

"I did it," she said. Her eyes shone. "I rode my bike!"

# 9. The Purple Panther

The next few days were teacher work days. There was no school, so Lilley had plenty of time to ride her bike.

Every morning after breakfast, Lilley strapped on her helmet and wheeled her bike out of the garage. Why had she ever been afraid? Her bike was a friend. Like a pet horse. She had even named it. The Purple Panther.

With Dad at work, Lilley had no one to hold the bike while she got on. So she invented her own method.

First, she swung her legs over the saddle. Next, she tiptoed the bike up the small hill by her driveway.

Then she put her left foot on the pedal and pushed off with her right foot, giving an extra push for luck.

The bike gathered speed. Lilley pumped, her feet flashing up and down, up and down. She leaned into the corner and turned with the road. A cool breeze whistled past her ears as she rode, and the wheels sang songs.

She hummed a tune she made up: "I'm riding, riding, really riding."

Over and over and over she sang, to the rhythm of the wheels on the ground.

Once, she took the corner too fast. The bike hit the curb and bounced up. Lilley and the bike crashed to the ground.

Lilley found a bloody spot on her elbow. She thought about putting the bike away.

But, in spite of crashing, she couldn't stop riding. She walked her bike home, where Mrs. Blick cleaned her wound.

"Coming in now, are you?" asked Mrs. Blick. She stuck a bandage on Lilley's elbow.

But Lilley shook her head. No stopping now. Not when it was such a thrill to sail up the street and down the street. Skimming like a swallow. Flying like a plane.

She dashed back outside. She strapped her helmet on and mounted up to ride again.

Red and brown leaves skittered across the street in front of her. Lilley raced the leaves down the street. The street was quiet. All the grown-ups were at work. Most of the kids were in day care. There was only Lilley and the leaves. And one yellow-eyed cat crouched under a bush, watching.

On Friday, Lilley asked Dad if she could ride to Adam's house.

Dad smiled. "Certainly, Lilley. Remember to ride on the right."

She called him on the phone to tell him she was coming. "I have something to show you," she said.

"Cool," said Adam. There was a pause. "Then we're friends again?"

"Of course," said Lilley, surprised. In all the excitement of learning to ride, she'd forgotten about their argument.

"Great," said Adam. "See you."

It was exciting to be riding someplace real. Lilley signaled for a turn at the corner.

Soon she spotted Adam's house. Adam circled on his big black bike.

Sally rode a tricycle with a red wagon tied on behind. She wore her cape with the S on back.

"I have superpowers," Sally told Lilley. "Want to see?"

Lilley put on her coaster brakes. She put her foot down before the bike could topple.

"Okay."

"Geez, Louise," said Adam. He pushed his glasses up. "You don't either have superpowers, Sal. Give it up."

"Do so," said Sally.

"Do not," said Adam.

Sally ignored Adam. She turned to Lilley. "I will now magic that bird into a white rabbit," said Sally.

She pointed to a sparrow hopping along the sidewalk.

Sally got off her tricycle. She picked up a stick. She twirled. The cape flew out behind her. Suddenly she stopped and pointed the stick.

"Abracadabra!" she chanted. "Be a bird!"

The bird looked at her with its bright eye and flew into a tree. Sally smirked.

"See?" she told brother. "Do so have superpowers. I turned that rabbit into a bird, didn't I?"

Adam snorted. "Super Sally, you said you were going to turn the bird into a rabbit. It already was a bird. You didn't do anything."

But Lilley was charmed. She wished she had a little sister. She clapped. Sally gave her brother a look and bowed.

Adam rolled his eyes. "Can you make yourself invisible now?"

But Sally was already pedaling down to the end of the block, singing magic songs without words.

Adam turned to Lilley.

"So," said Adam. "You can ride, huh? Cool bike."

Lilley climbed on her bike and rode in a slow circle to show him. Adam strapped his helmet on and chased her. Looping and swooping, they rode down the street. Adam followed Lilley. Lilley followed Adam. It was like a bike rodeo.

At first, it was hard for Lilley to keep up. But soon they both rode fast, yelling each time they passed, "Bread and butter! Bread and butter!"

By the end of the afternoon, Lilley rode almost as well as Adam. They agreed to meet Monday morning at Adam's house. They would ride their bikes to school together.

"No more buses, no more books," yelled Lilley.

"No more Maureen's dirty looks!" sang Adam.

Cool, thought Lilley as she pedaled home. No more mean Maureen.

# 10. Green Eyes

But on Monday, everything went wrong.

Lilley's alarm clock didn't go off.

Dad pounded on her door. "Get going, Tiger," he told her. "You don't want to be late." He gave her a kiss and took off for work, leaving behind a smell of shaving lotion.

Lilley struggled out of bed. She pulled on her striped socks. She couldn't find her favorite T-shirt. She pulled on a shirt from the floor.

Mrs. Blick banged around the kitchen. She wasn't wearing any earrings at all. Always a bad sign. She frowned at Lilley.

"In this house, we do not wear dirty playclothes to school," she said.

And Lilley had to go upstairs and change.

When she came down again, Mrs. Blick shoved a bowl of oatmeal at her.

"None of that sugar garbage today," she grumped. "Not on a school morning. You need a good solid breakfast that'll stick to your ribs."

The oatmeal tasted like old sneakers. Lilley pushed her bowl away.

"I've got to go," she said. "I can't be late!"

She grabbed her backpack and helmet and ran out the door before Mrs. Blick could stop her.

Lilley climbed on her bike. Push, push. She sailed past the houses on her street. Down the block, around the corner, and up one block to Adam's house.

Sally was out front, wearing her cape and riding her tricycle.

Maybe Adam is late, too, thought Lilley. She put down her kickstand.

"Adam's gone," Sally sang. "I magicked him into a rabbit and he hopped away, good day. I magicked him into a bird and he flew away, today."

Lilley shook her head. "Stop singing, Sally. Where's Adam?"

Mrs. Levy came out on the front porch. "Sally! Time for preschool! Come wash your face."

She saw Lilley. "Oh, Lilley! Adam thought you must have taken the bus after all. He was afraid he'd be late. He left a little while ago."

Lilley pressed her lips together. It was too late to catch the bus. She could ask Mrs. Blick to drive her, but she was pretty grumpy today.

Or she could ride to school by herself.

But that was okay, wasn't it? Dad said she could ride with Adam, but surely he'd understand she had to go by herself. And she could come home with Adam.

"I can drop you off when I take Sally to pre-school," Mrs. Levy told her.

Lilley shook her head. "No thanks, Mrs. Levy. I'll ride."

Mrs. Levy nodded. "Fine. Have a good day!"

She scooped Sally up and hauled her inside.

Lilley threw her leg over the seat. Push, push. She started off again. She knew the way.

She'd never been so late. The streets were quiet and empty. No kids riding bikes. No kids walking. No kids waiting for the bus.

She pedaled faster. Her helmet felt light, but her backpack grew heavier.

Turn right at the next block. Or was it left? She was almost sure it was right.

This block was familiar. She sighed with relief. Now she knew where she was! Only two blocks to go! In the distance, she heard the buzzer, calling the kids from the playground. She put on a burst of speed. Maybe she wouldn't be late after all.

Bruno's house loomed up ahead. For a moment, she turned icy cold. Not to worry. He'd be tied up. Wouldn't he?

She threw her weight against the pedals, willing the bike forward. Her breath came in gasps. Almost past.

A dark shape lunged from the yard. Bruno streaked beside Lilley, nipping at her ankle. His teeth closed on her pants leg and ripped.

Lilley pulled her feet out of the way. The bike wobbled in a big circle. She struggled to keep it steady. She couldn't fall off. She just couldn't.

"Bruno!"

Lilley heard a shout, but didn't look back. The barks got fainter. The dog was gone.

Lilley stopped back at the corner. She leaned against the stop sign and closed her eyes. Sweat ran under her helmet. Her knees shook.

When she felt better, she examined her leg. No blood. Only a jagged tear from Bruno's teeth. Good thing she wasn't wearing leggings!

Now what? She couldn't get to school that way. She could not—could not—ride past that house again. There must be some other way.

She closed her eyes to picture the road. If she went around the block, she'd miss Bruno's house. Then she could turn left. And there would be the school. She hoped.

Her heart stopped pounding. She looked both ways and walked her bike across the street. Then she got on.

It was hard work pedaling up the hill. She pressed all her weight down on the pedals.

This street was steeper than it looked. This part of town looked different, too. The houses were smaller, with tiny front yards and no trees. The road had more holes, too, and there were no sidewalks.

She stopped at a stop sign. Turn right, she told herself. She signaled and turned.

And screeched to a stop.

The road in front of her swooped down, down, down in a long, steep hill. At the bottom of the hill a flagpole glistened. The school!

But that hill! She'd never seen such a steep hill! She couldn't ride down a hill like that. It was too much! She couldn't bear it. She wasn't a tiger after all. Just a cowardly lion.

Tears filled her eyes. She didn't see a girl open the door and run across the lawn. She didn't see, until the girl grabbed Lilley's handlebars.

Lilley looked up.

Mean green eyes drilled into her.

"Where do you think you're going, pip-squeak?"

It was Maureen.

# 11. Pink Bunnies

Maureen gripped the handlebars of Lilley's bike.

Lilley gasped. Maureen shoved her face close to Lilley's. Maureen's face was so pale, her freckles looked red. No, wait. Those weren't freckles. Those were . . .

"Chicken pox!"

A flush of red crept over Maureen's cheeks. "So what?" she said. "Want to make something of it?"

A lump the size of a meatball formed in Lilley's throat. She was going to get creamed, and there was no way out. No way at all.

Behind her lay the steepest, longest hill she had ever seen. And in front of her was Maureen. Mean,

mean, green Maureen. And Maureen would never let her pass.

Lilley tried to swallow, but nothing went down. She stared at Maureen and Maureen stared back. Lilley saw the red chicken pox spots. The green eyes. The pink bunnies on her nightgown.

Pink bunnies. The meatball in Lilley's throat began to shrink. What kind of bully wears pink bunnies? Why, Maureen's just a bossy old fourth-grader with chicken pox! I had chicken pox when I was three. And pink bunnies! I wear pink bunnies, thought Lilley. And I'm a wimp!

No, not a wimp. I can do thirty chin-ups. I can ride a two-wheeler.

Lilley's heart beat like a drum. What had Maureen actually done to her, anyway? Practically nothing! Called her a few names. Threatened to cream her. Shaken her fist.

Oh, Maureen was a bully all right. A mean, bossy girl. But Adam was right. Sometimes you just have to stand up for yourself.

Lilley looked Maureen straight in her green eyes.

"Let go," she ordered. "I'm late for school!" She yanked her bike away.

Surprised, Maureen stepped back. She dug her fists into her hips. She glared. "You can't ride down that hill," she said. "You'll crash. Even I don't ride down that hill!"

But Lilley didn't stop.

"See you at school, Maureen!" she yelled.

And she climbed aboard her bike.

# 12. What Happened Next

Lilley zoomed down the hill on her bike. Houses, trees, and fences whizzed past. Faster and faster.

She clung to her bike for dear life, forgetting all about her coaster brakes. It was terrifying. It was wonderful.

The wind whistled in her ears. It stung her cheeks. The tires hummed against the road, spinning, spinning. Lilley soared like an eagle, roaring to school.

I'm free! I can fly! I can ride a bike. I can do thirty chin-ups. I can conquer a bully!

"I'm Tiger Lilley!" she yelled. And the words blew away in the wind.

At last the hill flattened out. The bike slowed. Lilley braked to a stop by the school flagpole. The bell had rung. The playground was deserted.

With unsteady hands, Lilley unfastened her helmet. She set the kickstand. She sat down on the curb in front of the school to let her heart slow and her knees stop trembling.

She looked back up the steep hill she'd just ridden down. *I rode down that? Wow! Wait till I tell Adam!*

A car pulled up. Cassandra got out. Her mouth looked puffy. "New filling," she mumbled when she saw Lilley.

"You look awful!" she told Lilley. "What happened? Did Maureen beat you up?"

Lilley laughed. All this time she thought Cassandra was the voice of doom. But really she was even more scared of Maureen than Lilley herself.

"I rode my bike," she said. And pointed.

Cassandra's eyes went wide. "Down *that* hill? You?"

"Sure," she said. "No sweat." She chained her bike to the rack. Let's go get our late passes."

Cassandra's shoulders drooped. "I hate getting a late pass. Everyone stares."

Lilley put her arm around Cassandra's shoulders. "I'll take you in," she said.

After school, Lilley and Adam rode home together, taking the shortcut Adam knew, the one without hills, or dogs, or Maureen.

Adam's eyes went big behind his glasses when Lilley told him about her wild ride.

"Wow!" he said. "It's like I told you, Lilley. You aren't a wimp."

He shook his head in disbelief. "Bruno, Maureen, the bike, thirty chin-ups. Wow!"

## What Happened Next

. . .

Lilley sat on her bed. She wore her pj's with the pink bunnies. Just like Maureen's nightgown. She giggled a little as she thought of Maureen's face right before she rode down the hill.

She looked at a new tiger Dad had given her. He was stuffed with beans, and small enough to fit in her palm. He had pale blue wings. He made her think of flying. Of riding her bike down the hill.

Lilley smiled, remembering. Tomorrow, she and Adam would ride to school.

But in the winter, when it rained or snowed, she wouldn't be afraid to ride the bus.

Not now. Not Tiger Lilley.

# Lilley's Bicycle Safety Tips

Tiger Lilley's dad belongs to a bicycle club. He taught Lilley a lot about bicycle safety. Here are some of Lilley's safety tips:

## Wear a safety helmet

Everyone should always wear a bicycle helmet. Many states require them. Even if your state doesn't, bicycle helmets are smart. They protect your head from injury.

The helmet must fit properly or it won't do any good. Put the helmet on so it covers the top of your head. Tighten the straps. Push the helmet back and forth. It should not move. If the helmet moves, it's too loose. You can buy soft pads to put inside the helmet to make it fit snugly.

## Keep to the right

When Lilley rode her tricycle, she stayed on the sidewalk. Now that she can ride a two-wheeler, she rides on the road. She knows she must always ride in the same direction cars drive. She rides on the right hand side of the road. That way, drivers can see Lilley and see her hand signals.

## Use hand signals

It's important to let drivers know when you are going to turn. Cars cannot stop as fast as bicycles, so you have to let them know in plenty of time. Other cyclists need to know as well. Hand signals let everyone know what you're going to do.

All hand signals are made with the left arm. It can be tricky to steer with just your right hand. Lilley practiced her hand signals on a quiet street before she rode in traffic.

## Lilley's Bicycle Safety Tips

To make a left turn, hold your left arm straight out.

To signal a right turn, put your left arm up.

To stop, hold your left arm down.

## Walk across intersections

When Lilley comes to a street corner, she dismounts. She holds her bicycle between her body and traffic. She looks both ways before walking her bicycle across the street.

## Obey traffic signs

Bicycles share the road with cars, trucks, motor-cycles, and pedestrians. Bicyclists need to obey traffic signs. Lilley stops at the stop sign on her corner. When she rides downtown with Dad, they stop on red lights and go on green. Because a bike is not as fast as a car, Dad always stops for yellow lights as well. "It's best to be safe," he tells Lilley.

## Ride in a single file

Now that Lilley has learned to ride a two-wheeler, she rides to school with Adam. They always ride single file. That makes it easy for cars to get around them. At first, Adam always wanted to be in front. "That's not fair, Adam," Lilley told him. Now they take turns.

## Lilley's Bicycle Safety Tips

There's a lot of traffic in front of the school before and after school. Lilley and Adam walk their bikes through the parking lot.

Lilley enjoys riding her bicycle so much now, she wants to join Dad's bicycle club!

**The End**